Illustrations, copyright © 1978 Tony Hutchings.
Text, copyright © 1978 Rand McNally & Company.
Printed in the United States of America by Rand McNally & Company
ISBN 0-528-82238-1
    0-528-80062-0 lib. bdg.
Library of Congress Catalog Card Number 78-17854

# Silly Dinosaurs

**Illustrated by Hutchings**

Rand McNally & Company    Chicago · New York · San Francisco

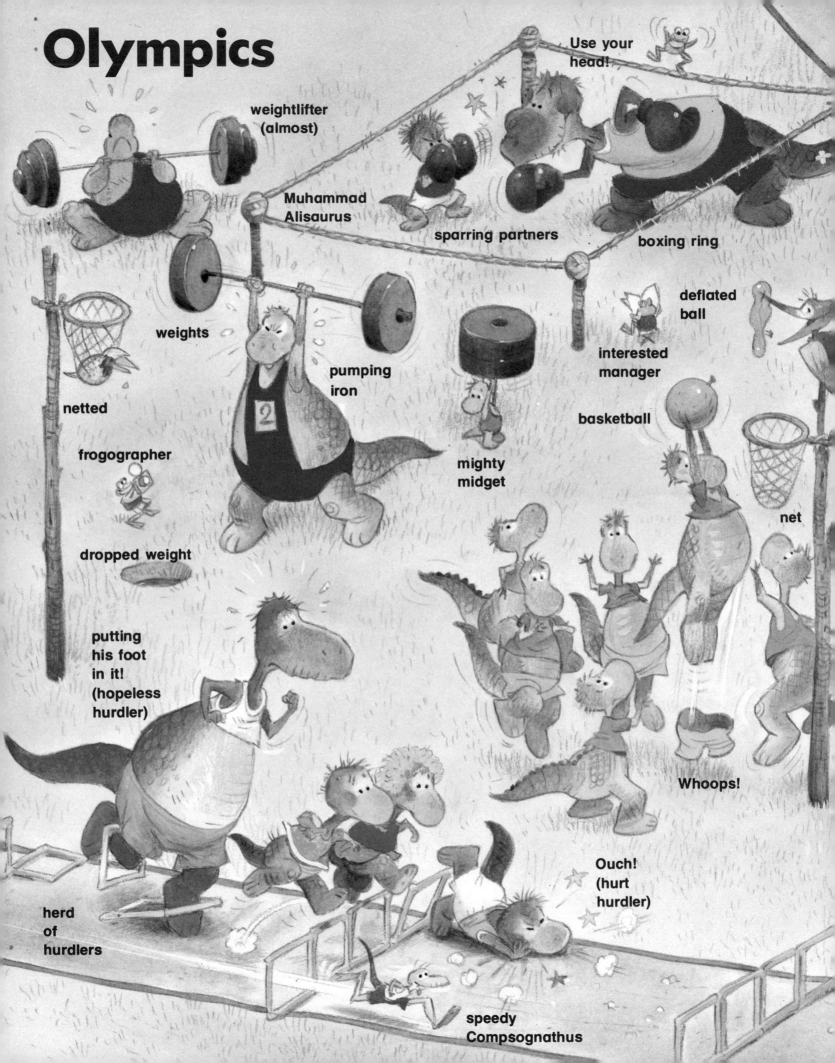

spider web

professor ookasaurus

window

ssel

teacher's pet

pointer

Polly Frog

cactus

polliwog

inky splot

easel

chalk board

munched board

sick caterpillar

daydreamer

paw print

apple

new pupil

popgun

pet crocodile

balloon

drip

ball

Teacher took the toys.

some surprises

NURSERY SCHOOL

broken glasses

another yo-yo

stool

inky footprints

PERSONAL HYGIENE TIPS
Eat 150 lb. green vegetables or
3½ trees daily.
Floss your fangs daily.
Clip your claws.
Keep claws clean.
Polish your scales.

# A Dinosaur in the Meadow

*by Betty Lacey*

Once upon a time, when the earth was quite young, a small dinosaur awakened one day from his nap. He crawled out of the deep, dark cave where he had been sleeping for a million years and a day. He yawned, as small dinosaurs liked to do, and he stretched.

He blinked in the sunshine. Everything was peaceful and still. He looked around. Not another dinosaur was in sight.

He sniffed a daisy. He nibbled at the topmost leaves of a gingko tree. He picked a buttercup and held it under his chin to see if he liked butter. But he couldn't see if the buttercup made a yellow shadow. And there was nobody there to tell him.

He sat on a log. "There's nothing to do," he said. And he didn't like that at all.

Just then an orange and black butterfly flitted past him, dipping from flower to flower. She looked so happy that the little dinosaur thought, "I would like to do that."

So he followed her, flapping his arms and trying his best to flit. *Galumph, galumph, galumph.*

The orange and black butterfly was amazed, and she flew home as fast as she could.

"Mother, Mother," she said. "There is a dinosaur in the meadow and he is trying to flit from flower to flower."

"Nonsense, dear," said her mother. "It must be your imagination. Dinosaurs do not flit."

Strangely enough, that's exactly what the small dinosaur had decided. Flitting was not to his taste. He didn't seem to do it quite right. And he didn't feel as happy as the orange and black butterfly.

He drew circles in the dust with his toe. Lots and lots of circles. It wasn't much fun, not having anything to do.

Soon a gazelle went leaping past him.

The small dinosaur watched. She looked so pleased with what she was doing that he thought, "I would like to do that."

So he went leaping after her. *Kalumph, kalumph, kalumph.*

The gazelle was so astonished that she went leaping home and said, "Father, Father, there's a dinosaur in the meadow and he is jumping and leaping."

"Oh, my, no," said her father. "It must be your imagination, my pet. Dinosaurs do not jump and leap."

By that time, the small dinosaur had decided that very thing for himself. He didn't feel pleased with leap- ing. And besides, he had bumped his head. He sat in the shade of a tree and rubbed his chin. And, oh how he wished for something to do. It was simply terrible not to have something to do.

At that moment he spied a badger busily digging a hole under a rock. The dirt flew as she used her long nails to dig, dig, dig. And she hummed a cheerful song.

"Now that," the small dinosaur decided, "is something I would really like to do. I'll make a hole as big as me."

He scraped at the dirt with one foot and then with the other. But he did not have long badger nails. *Scrumph, scrumph, scrumph.* All he did was make clouds of dust.

The badger watched him in wonderment. Then she went running home. "Grandmother, Grandfather," she said, "There is a dinosaur in the meadow and I think he is trying to dig a hole. But he is not doing it very well."

"Mercy me," said the old badger grandmother. "You are imagining things, love."

Her grandfather laughed. "Oh, ho, ho. Dinosaurs do not dig holes. Oh, no, no, no."

The small dinosaur had already learned that. He settled down in the dirt and tears dripped down his dusty cheeks. "Well, I wish there really was something to do," he said.

Just then there was a rustling in the grass and a crocodile came thumping past. "I see," he said, "you have been rolling in the dirt, and that is fine. But for myself, I would much rather roll in the mud. Let me show you where the mud is thick and oozy." He made it sound very inviting.

So the small dinosaur wiped his eyes and followed the crocodile to the edge of a lake where the mud was just as the crocodile had described it. The crocodile smiled as he sank deep into the cool ooze.

But the small dinosaur was not even watching him, for he was staring at the lake beyond. Water bugs made ripples on the blue water. Gentle waves went *slap, slap, slap.*

He skipped past the crocodile and dove into the cool water. He spattered and he sputtered and he splashed. And he laughed the whole time he did it.

Nearby, a head came out of the water. "Hello," said a not very big dinosaur. "My name is Desmond. Want to play?"

There was an enormous splash and another head rose out of the water. "Hi," said another not very big dinosaur. "My name is Esmond and I can blow bubbles. Can you blow bubbles?"

So they all blew bubbles.

On the shore, everyone watched the small dinosaur splash and swim and tread water.

"Amazing," said the orange and black butterfly.

"Astonishing," said the gazelle.

"Wonderful," said the badger.

Together they all sighed, "I wish I could do that."

But the crocodile said nothing at all. For he was fast asleep in the cool mud.

The small dinosaur floated on his back with his
friends. He was happy, he was pleased, he was cheerful.
He had found the very best of all things to do.

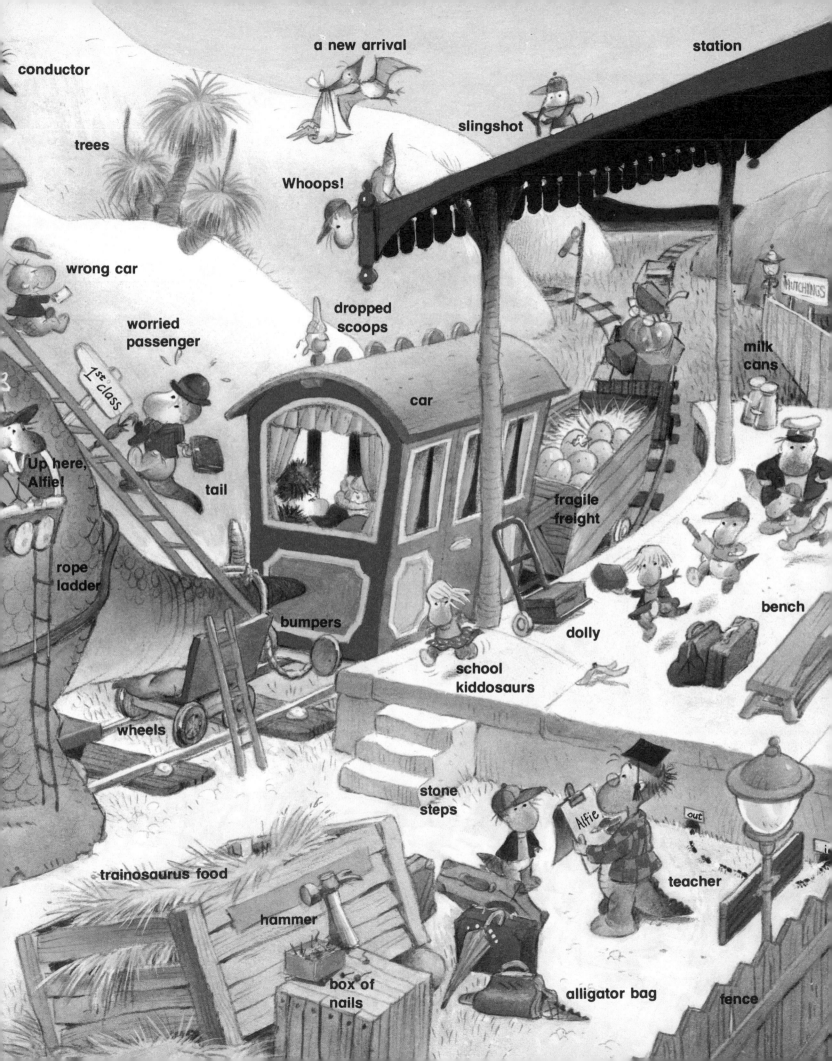

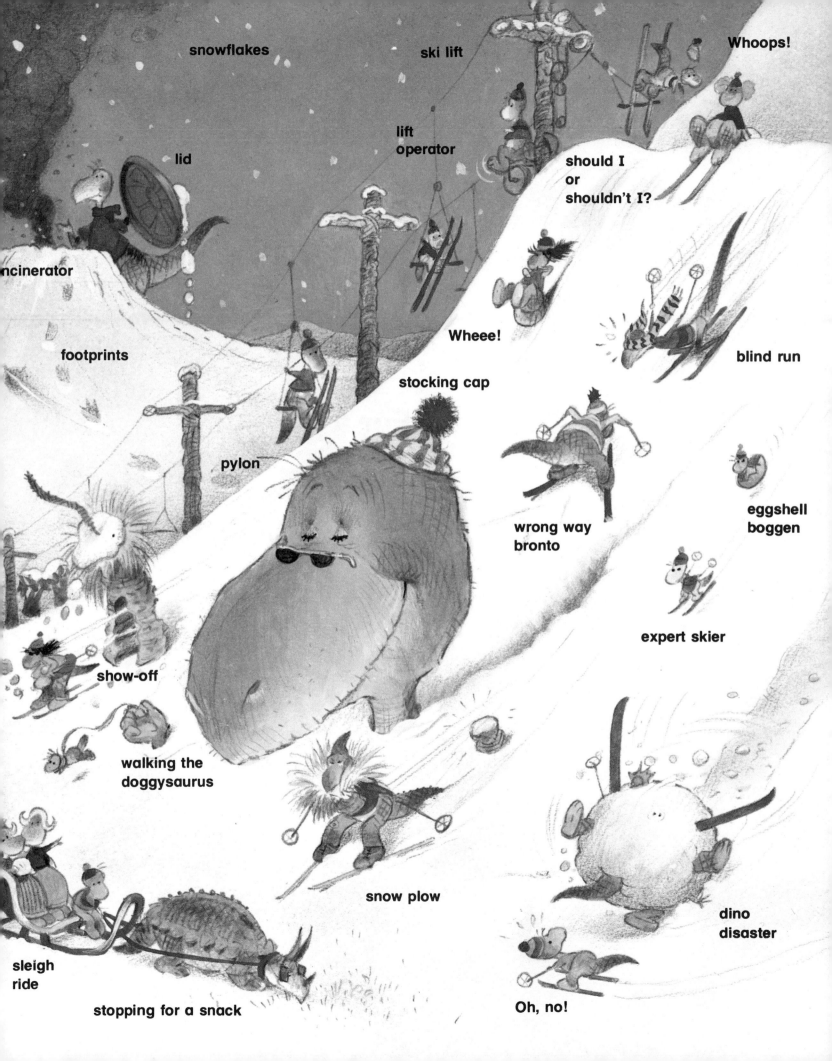

# Dinosaur For a Day

by *Charlotte Herman*

One day, Michael sat down to read his latest copy of his favorite magazine, *Dinosaur Digest*. On page 1 there was a picture of a huge, green dinosaur, and under the picture were these words:

**WIN DUFFY THE DINOSAUR**
**For A Day**

**Duffy is so real you won't believe your eyes!**
**Just complete this sentence in twenty-five words or less:**
**I would like to spend a day with a dinosaur because...**

Michael loved dinosaurs and he loved contests, so he decided to enter right away.

He could think of lots of things to write. He could write how he'd like to spend a day with a dinosaur because he had never met a dinosaur before, or because he could ride him to school, or because green was his favorite color.

But the main reason Michael wanted a dinosaur was because he loved them more than any other animal in the world. So he got some paper and on page 1 he wrote: I would like to spend a day with a dinosaur because I love dinosaurs more than any other animal in the world.

Then he counted up his words to make sure he had twenty-five or less, and he tore the page out of the magazine and sent it away with his letter.

"I just entered a dinosaur contest," he told his mother. "If I win I get to spend a whole day with a dinosaur."

"Well, I hope you *do* win," his mother said. "But remember, it might take many months before they decide on a winner. So you'll have to be patient."

The next day there was a knock on the door. Michael stood on a chair so he could look through the peephole to see who it was. All he could see was green. "Maybe it's my dinosaur," said Michael. "Maybe I won the contest." He climbed off the chair and opened the door.

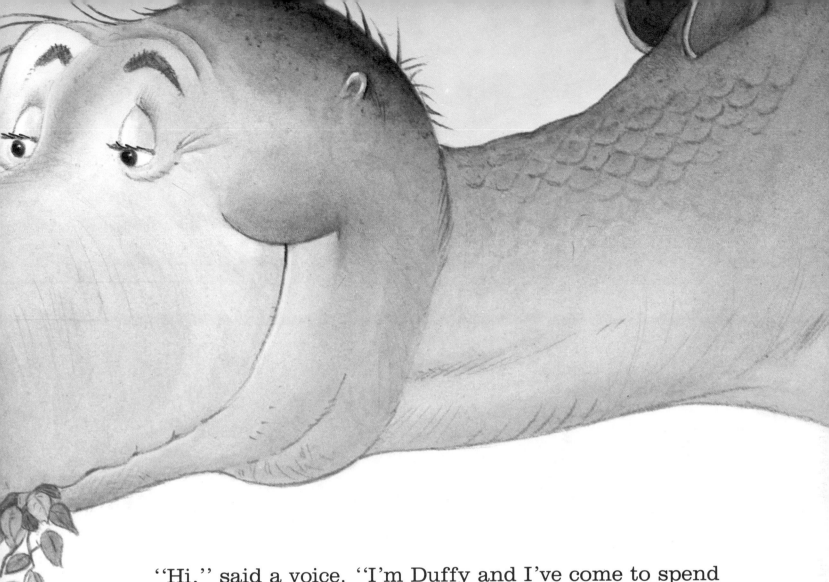

"Hi," said a voice. "I'm Duffy and I've come to spend the day with you."

"I won!" shouted Michael, jumping up and down. "I really won." He looked up at Duffy. "Wow! You sure do look real."

"That's because I *am* real," said Duffy.

Duffy was too large to fit through the doorway. So he had to stay outside while Michael introduced him to his mother.

"You're just in time," said Michael's mother. "I have an important appointment and I need a sitter. Do you think you can drop me off downtown?"

Duffy lowered his head so that Michael and his mother could climb on top of him. As they rode along, they waved to all their friends and neighbors.

"They must be having company from out of town," said one neighbor to another.

"That sure beats driving," said a man whose car had broken down.

Up on top of Duffy, Michael could feel a cool summer breeze. "This is more fun than the bus," he said.

Every once in a while Duffy stopped to eat some leaves from the trees. Pretty soon they reached the building where Michael's mother had her appointment. Duffy let her in through a window so she wouldn't have to take the elevator all the way up to the tenth floor.

"Thanks for the ride," she said.

"Where to now?" asked Duffy.

"How about the amusement park?" said Michael. "That's always a fun place."

When they reached the amusement park, they saw a long line of children waiting for pony rides. "Oh, good," said Michael. "I don't have to wait for a pony." And he rode Duffy around the pony track five times.

After the ride, Michael and Duffy ate cotton candy and ice cream. "This tastes better than leaves," said Duffy.

Duffy looked around the park and pointed to a game booth. "Hey, look at all those baby dinosaurs over there."

Michael laughed. "Those are just toy dinosaurs. They're prizes. Let's try to win one."

A little girl pointed at Duffy. "That's the prize I want," she yelled. "I want that big one."

"Sorry," said Duffy. "But I'm not a prize."

"What do we have to do to win one of these dinosaurs?" Michael asked the man in the game booth.

"I have to guess your weight. And if I can't, then you're the winner," said the man.

"Okay," said Michael. "Guess my weight."

The man felt Michael's arms and legs, and then he turned him around a few times. "Thirty-five pounds," he said.

Michael got up on the scale. The pointer pointed to thirty-five pounds. "Sorry," said the man. "I guessed your weight, so no prize for you."

"Now guess *my* weight," said Duffy.

The man felt Duffy's foot and tried to turn him around. He couldn't move him. "Thirty thousand pounds," he guessed.

"Wrong," said Duffy. "I weigh forty thousand pounds."

"I guess I'll have to take your word for it," said the man, and he gave Duffy a dinosaur that looked just like Duffy.

Michael and Duffy walked over to a booth where a photographer was taking pictures. ''I'd love to have our picture taken,'' said Michael. ''But I don't have any money left in my pockets.''

''And I don't have any pockets,'' said Duffy.

''That's all right,'' said the photographer. ''I'd be honored to take your picture for nothing. I've never taken a picture of a dinosaur before.''

The photographer told Michael and Duffy that they could choose whatever scene they wanted for a background. Duffy chose a swamp scene because it reminded him of home.

After their picture was taken, Michael and Duffy
heard a loud commotion coming from the roller coaster.
They ran to see what was going on. A large crowd was
gathering around the roller coaster, which was stuck
way up on top of the tracks. People were yelling from the
top.

"Hurry up and get us down," called a voice. "I'm hungry."

"Have no fear, Duffy is here," said Duffy. "I'll get you down."

Duffy stood next to the roller coaster. "Climb aboard and slide down my back," he told everyone.

One by one, the people climbed on top of Duffy and slid down his back. "Hurray for Duffy!" the people shouted. "He got us down and gave us a ride at the same time."

They wanted to pick him up and sing "For He's a Jolly Good Fellow," but he was too big and heavy. So they had a parade instead, with Duffy and Michael leading the way.

It was starting to get dark. All the lights in the amusement park were turned on. "I'd better take you home," said Duffy. "It's getting late."

"It's too bad you have to go away soon," said Michael as they rode home together.

"I know," said Duffy. "But I have to. I'm only for a day."

When they reached Michael's house, Duffy made sure that Michael's mother was home, and then he said good-bye.

"You can have the baby dinosaur to remember me by."

"Thank you," said Michael. "And you can have the picture to remember me by."

Duffy walked off into the night. "Don't forget me," he called.

"I won't," said Michael.

*How could anyone forget a forty-thousand-pound dinosaur?* Michael wondered. Especially a forty-thousand-pound dinosaur who was also a friend. Because that's what Michael and Duffy were. Friends. And not just for a day, either. Michael knew they would be friends for always.

# Gas Station

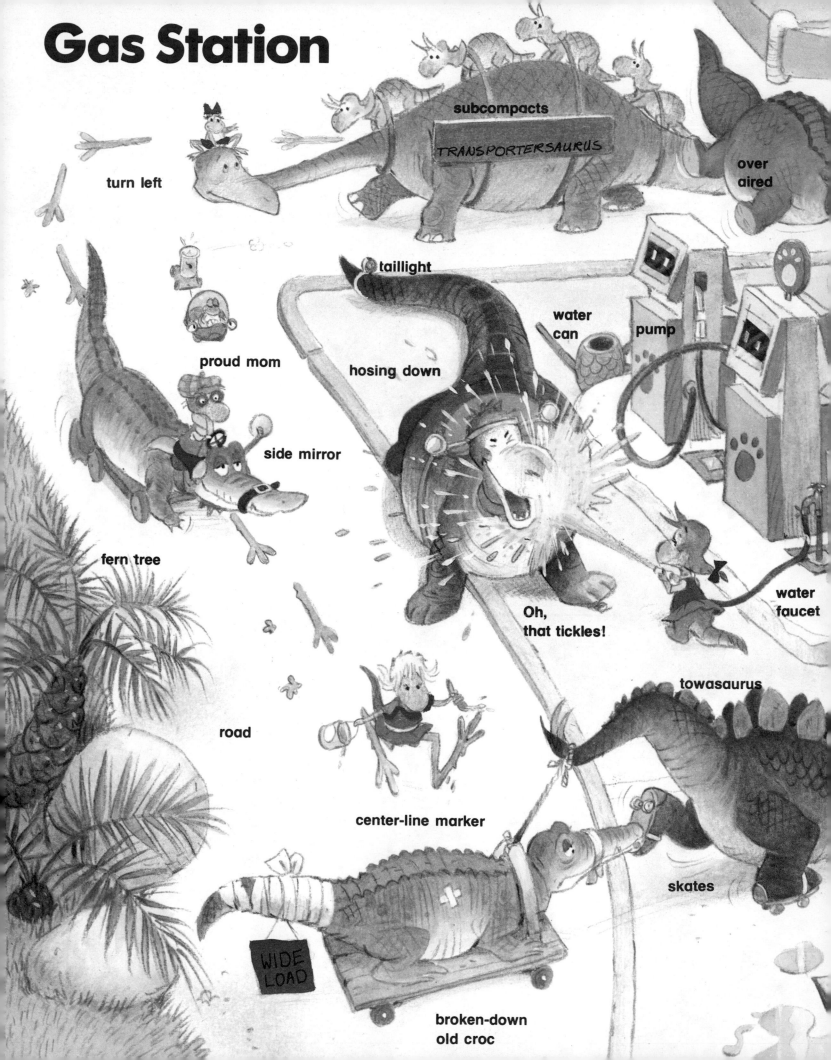

# Dinosaur Disco

The Pterodactyl Trio

maraca

spotlighter frog

shades

Roy Orbisaurus

all ri–ight!

Elvisaurus

medallion

muted trumpet

jacket

bow tie

beret

organist

speaker

T-shirt

The Wiggle

Pterodactyl Twist

Bronto Bump

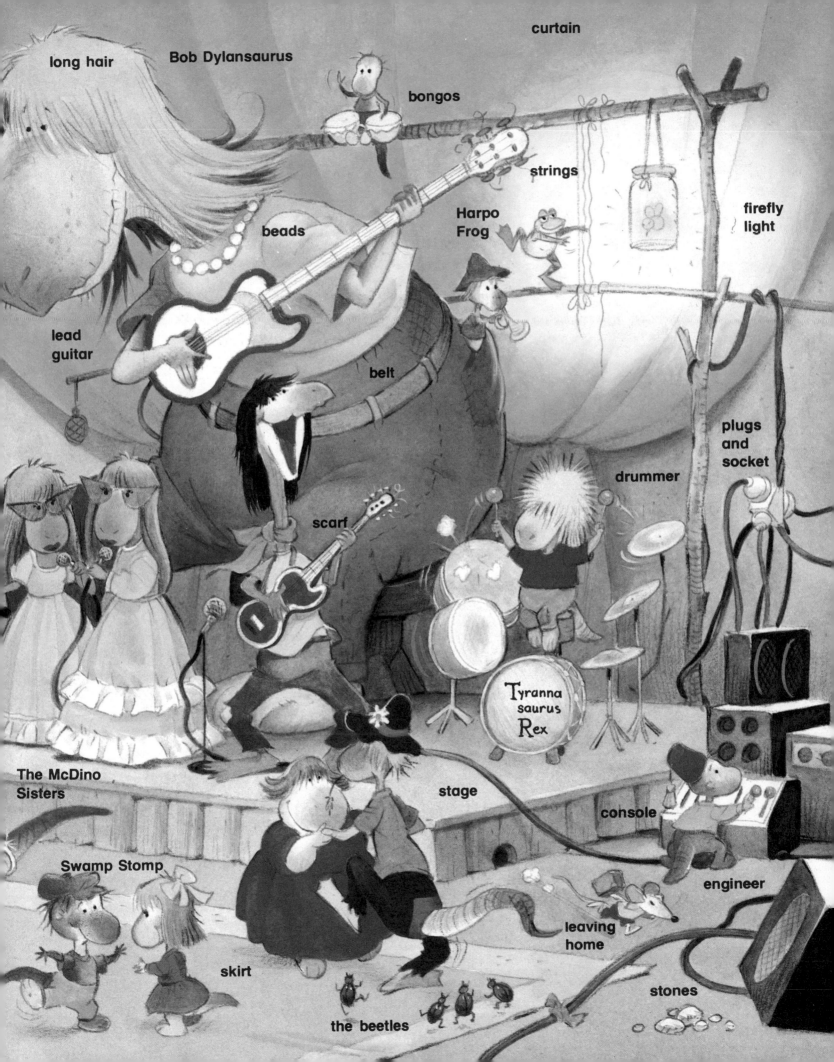

# Family Pictures